To Wesley, Lucy, Wendy, and Juniper—
being your dad has been better than a whole
universe made of pizza.
—K. S.

To my son Hugo, for whom in a heartbeat
I would turn the entire universe into pizza!
—A. P.

A Pizza with EVERYTHING ON IT

BY
KYLE SCHEELE

ILLUSTRATED BY
ANDY J. PIZZA

chronicle books·san francisco

When your dad owns a pizza shop, you can have whatever kind of pizza you want.

So when Dad asked what I was hungry for, I said, "Give me a pizza with EVERYTHING on it."

Dad said, "Everything?"
I said, "EVERYTHING."

Dad tossed the dough while I
stirred the sauce.

We put down three different kinds of cheese,
then added a fourth . . . just to be safe.

CHEDDAR

SWISS

MOZZARELLA

MYSTERIOUS
4th CHEESE

We started with the basics:
Pepperoni. Sausage.
Tomatoes. Peppers.
Even those little mushrooms that
look like noses.

Dad said, "Perfect!"

But I said, "No, Dad! I want a pizza with
EVERYTHING on it!"

Dad ran across the street and came back with his arms full of groceries.

PICKLES

ICE CREAM CONE

BOILED EGGS

APPLE

AN ENTIRE TURKEY

BAG OF CHIPS

All of it went on the pizza.

Dad said, "Perfect!"

But I said, "No, Dad! I want a
pizza with EVERYTHING on it!"

In a flash, Dad threw his rolling pin onto the pizza, followed by his chef's hat. I put the blender on top as Dad added a table and chairs.

Books, pencils, and a notebook fell onto the pizza
as I turned my backpack upside down.

Dad said, "Perfect!"

But I said, "No, Dad!
I want a pizza with
EVERYTHING on it!"

Dad said, "I think we're going to
need to take this outside."

Dad rolled the pizza into the street as I rode my bicycle up onto the toppings.

Dad added a doghouse.

Then a tree house.

Then a real house.

Then the White House!

But something was about to go TERRIBLY wrong.

Perhaps it was the addition of the particle accelerator . . .

or perhaps the weight of the pizza simply became greater than what the crust could bear.

Whatever it was, it was BAD.

Just as Dad was pushing the wheelbarrow full of penguins to the top of the pizza, there was a loud **POP!**

In the blink of an eye,
the pizza began to collapse
in on itself.

EVERYTHING was speeding
towards the center of the pizza.

I grabbed Dad's hand. Dad grabbed the crust. We held on for dear life.

"It's a pizza black hole!" Dad shouted. "Everything is being sucked in!"

"Everything?" I yelled back. Dad gulped. "EVERYTHING!"

Dads are awfully strong,
but black holes are stronger.

Especially pizza black holes.

"I can't hang on anymore!" Dad yelled.

Together we flew into the swirling pizza vortex.

Then everything
went BLACK.

And everything STAYED black.

As black as burnt pizza crust.

Then BOOM!
A pizza big bang!

The universe exploded
in a burst of toppings.
EVERYTHING was pizza.

Dad and I were launched
through a pizza galaxy
and into our pizza
solar system.

We flew towards
a pizza earth . . .

into our pizza town.

We landed back at
our pizza shop.

Or should I say,
our PIZZA pizza shop.

Dad looked at me.
"Perfect?" he said, a little unsure.

Library of Congress Cataloging-in-Publication Data available.

ISBN 978-1-7972-0281-5

Manufactured in Canada.

Design by Jay Marvel.
Typeset in Steagal Rough.
The illustrations in this book were rendered in
gouache, pencil, and digital collage.

10 9 8 7 6 5 4 3

Chronicle books and gifts are available at special quantity discounts to corporations,
professional associations, literacy programs, and other organizations.
For details and discount information, please contact our premiums department at
corporatesales@chroniclebooks.com or at 1-800-759-0190.

Chronicle Books LLC
680 Second Street
San Francisco, California 94107

Chronicle Books—we see things differently.
Become part of our community at www.chroniclekids.com.